EGMONT

We bring stories to life

First published in Great Britain in 2007 by Dean,
an imprint of Egmont UK Limited
239 Kensington High Street, London W8 6SA

Thomas the Tank Engine & Friends™

A BRITT ALLCROFT COMPANY PRODUCTION

Based on The Railway Series by The Reverend W Awdry
Photographs © 2007 Gullane (Thomas) LLC. A HIT Entertainment Company

Thomas the Tank Engine & Friends and Thomas & Friends are trademarks of Gullane (Thomas) Limited.
Thomas the Tank Engine & Friends and Design is Reg. US. Pat. & Tm. Off.

ISBN 978 0 6035 6254 9
ISBN 0 6035 6254 X
1 3 5 7 9 10 8 6 4 2
Printed in Singapore

Emily's New Coaches

The Thomas TV Series

The engines were excited because a new engine was joining the Sodor Railway.

When Thomas came to Knapford Station he saw Emily, the new engine, waiting there. She was very smart with shiny brass fittings.

"Hello, I'm Thomas," wheeshed Thomas.

"Hello, I'm Emily," said the new engine.

Thomas picked up his passengers and said goodbye to Emily.

Then The Fat Controller said to her, "Your new coaches are arriving at the Docks today. I want you to learn the passenger routes before they get here, so go out and collect any coaches you find and bring them back here."

"I will do that right away, Sir," said Emily.

The only coaches Emily and her Driver could find were Annie and Clarabel.

"Let's take these coaches back to the station," said Emily's Driver.

Annie and Clarabel were cross.

"It should be Thomas pulling us, not this strange new train," said Annie to Clarabel, but Emily did not hear her.

When Edward passed Emily he went to whistle "Hello" but then he saw she was pulling Annie and Clarabel.

He thought she had stolen Thomas' coaches, so when Emily said "Hello" to him, he just stared crossly at her.

And when Percy passed her later, he also scowled at her.

Emily wondered why everyone was being so rude to her.

Then Thomas came along the line. Emily was pleased to see him because he had been so friendly that morning.

"Hello, Thomas," she said, cheerfully.

But to her surprise, Thomas glared at her and rushed past without saying a word.

Emily felt very sad. She thought no one liked her.

Later that day, The Fat Controller told Thomas to pick up the new coaches from the Docks.

"New coaches?" said Thomas. "But, I . . ."

"Really Useful Engines don't argue," said The Fat Controller, sternly.

Thomas set off grumpily. He didn't want *new* coaches, he wanted *his* coaches, Annie and Clarabel.

When Emily passed Tidmouth Sheds, Oliver said in surprise, "What are you doing with Thomas' coaches?"

"Oh!" said Emily. "*Now* I know why all the engines are so cross. The Fat Controller told me to pick up any coaches I could find, but I didn't realise these belong to Thomas. Everyone must think I've stolen them!"

Thomas collected the new coaches from the Docks.

They were shiny and smart, but Thomas didn't care.

"I don't want *new* coaches, I want *my* coaches!"
he said to himself.

He was cross because he thought Emily had stolen
Annie and Clarabel from him.

As Emily travelled to the station, a Signalman waved for her to stop.

"Oliver hasn't cleared his signal box," he said. "Please check what's wrong."

Oliver had broken down and was stuck on the crossing. Suddenly, Emily heard a whistle. Thomas was rushing towards Oliver.

He was braking hard, but he was going to crash into him!

Emily charged forward and with a burst of strength, pushed Oliver out of the way just in time.

Thomas came to a stop just behind her. He had had a lucky escape.

"Thank you," said Oliver. "You saved us from a really nasty accident."

"Yes, thank you," said Thomas, grumpily.

He was still upset because he thought Emily had taken his coaches.

"I haven't stolen your coaches," Emily said. "I am taking them to the station like the The Fat Controller asked me to."

"Oh!" peeped Thomas. Then he realised something.

"The new coaches I collected are for you, aren't they?" he asked.

"That's right!" laughed Emily. She was glad they were friends again.

"Hello," said Thomas when Emily met him at the yard later on. "I have a surprise for you!"

"A surprise? For me?" said Emily, excitedly.

"Yes. We are all really happy that you've joined our Railway so we're having a party to welcome you!"

"Oh, thank you!" said Emily.
She knew she was going to like working there with her new engine friends.